# Twelfth Night

Sweet Cherry
Publishing

Published by Sweet Cherry Publishing Limited
Unit E, Vulcan Business Complex,
Vulcan Road,
Leicester, LE5 3EB,
United Kingdom

First published in the USA in 2013
ISBN: 978-1-78226-081-3

©Macaw Books

Title: Twelfth Night
North American Edition

Text & Illustration by Macaw Books 2013

www.sweetcherrypublishing.com

Printed in the United Kingdom
Printed and Bound by CPI Group (UK) Ltd,
Croydon, CR0 4YY, UK

About
Shakespeare

William Shakespeare, regarded as the greatest writer in the English language, was born in Stratford-upon-Avon in Warwickshire, England (around April 23, 1564). He was the third of eight children born to John and Mary Shakespeare.

Shakespeare was a poet, playwright, and dramatist. He is often known as England's national poet and the "Bard of Avon." Thirty-eight plays, 154 sonnets, two long narrative poems, and several other poems are attributed to him. Shakespeare's plays have been translated into every major existent language and are performed more often than those of any other playwright.

Viola: Viola is the protagonist
of the play. She is the twin sister
of Sebastian and is in love with
the duke. After she is saved from
the shipwreck, she decides to
make her own way in the world
and serves the duke disguised
as a man called Cesario.

Olivia: She is a beautiful, wealthy lady. She is courted by the duke but does not welcome his advances because she is still mourning the deaths of her father and brother. However, she falls for Cesario, who is Viola in disguise.

Sebastian: He is Viola's twin brother. He is saved from the  shipwreck by a man called Antonio. Later in the play, Olivia wants to marry Sebastian, even though she has never met him.

Duke Orsino: Duke Orsino is a nobleman in Illyria. He is in love with Olivia, though she does not respond to his advances. He is also very fond of his page, Cesario, who is actually Viola.

Twelfth Night

There once lived a pair of twins, a brother and sister, called Sebastian and Viola. They belonged to the house of Messaline, a rather rich and noble family. They looked so

alike that if they were to wear each other's clothes, no one could tell the difference.

Once, when they went out sailing, they experienced one of the worst storms that had been seen in the recent past. As they approached the coast of Illyria, their ship capsized and was

shattered to pieces. The ship's
captain, along with some sailors,
were able to bail out in time and
reach the coastline safely. They
had managed to bring Viola with
them, but alas, the same could
not be said of Sebastian. Viola
was completely heartbroken. She
could not rejoice in the fact that

she had come out of the wreckage
alive and wept profusely for her
brother, who was presumed dead.

However, the ship's
captain offered her words of
consolation, declaring that as
the ship was breaking up, he
had seen Sebastian hold onto
a large mast and sail away. He

added that until he lost sight
of him, Sebastian had been
above water, and therefore,
he was confident he was still
alive. Viola was very happy
to hear the captain's report.

But now she was confronted
with another problem. She did
not know anything about the

alien land where she now found herself, nor did she know whom she could approach for assistance. But the captain was of help to her once again. He explained that he had been born not far from there and consequently knew the land well. He informed her that the land of Illyria was ruled by a rather noble duke by the name of Orsino.

Viola remembered her own father talking about Orsino and she commented that he was unmarried when her

father was alive. The captain
confirmed this to be true.
However, he also informed
her that Orsino was supposedly
madly in love with a fair damsel
called Olivia, and there was talk
about them getting married
very soon. But the captain also
went on to say that Olivia's

father and brother
had died recently,
which is why
she had refused
the company of men,
even the duke himself.

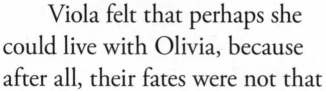

Viola felt that perhaps she
could live with Olivia, because
after all, their fates were not that
different; both
knew what it
was like to lose
a brother. But
again, the captain
declared that
Olivia had been
so heartbroken
after the death
of her brother,

that she seldom met anyone at
all, so perhaps she would refuse
to see Viola as well. Finally, it
was decided that Viola would
dress up as a man and take up
a job as the duke's page. That
seemed to be the only option
available to her at that moment.

The captain soon obtained
all the necessary clothes for Viola

and now she looked just like her
brother, Sebastian. The captain
took her with him to the court
of Orsino and introduced her
as the young Cesario. The duke
was impressed by the
young boy's gentle
appearance and
at once hired him
as his page. Soon

18

18

Cesario was able to impress the duke so much that he became his most favored attendant.

Therefore, it was Cesario in whom the duke confided about his love for Olivia. But therein lay the problem. As Orsino told Cesario, or rather Viola, about his love for Olivia, Viola herself fell in

love with the duke. She could not help thinking that the duke was truly a most noble man, loving a woman so much even though she shunned all his overtures.

One day she even threw him a subtle hint by asking whether he would accept the love of another woman who may have

fallen in love with him. But Orsino merely replied that no woman's heart was big enough to love  him the way he loved Olivia. He declared that it would be unfair to make any such comparison. Viola went on to mention a girl who once fell in love with a man, but was too afraid to declare her love for him. The duke was appalled at the story of the young girl, because he could see similarities in his own love for Olivia. But when he asked Cesario whether the girl died for love, Cesario decided that it was best to give

him an elusive answer
and let the matter rest.

While they were
still in conversation,
a man came into the
room and told the
duke that a note had
arrived from Olivia
stating that she could
not see the duke for
another seven years,
as she was still in a
period of mourning
for her late father and
brother. Only now did
the duke understand
the reason for her
not returning his
feelings of love. He

25

also commented that a woman who could love her brother and father so much that she could live a life of penance for seven years was definitely worthy of his love. He was overjoyed and decided that he must act.

He asked Cesario to go to Olivia's house at once and

stay there until she agreed to see him. If he were able to meet her, he should convince her that the duke was truly in love with the fair damsel.

Olivia's servants tried their best to send Cesario away, telling him that the mistress was not

well or that she was asleep. But Cesario, who did not like the job the duke had entrusted him with—for he was in love with the duke himself—had decided to carry out the job to the letter and refused to leave without seeing her. When Olivia

finally presented herself, there was
another problem that had to be
resolved, as Olivia immediately
fell in love with Cesario.

Cesario asked Olivia to
remove the veil that she had
draped over her face, and though
she was supposed to wear it
for the next seven years, at
Cesario's request she complied

immediately. Now that Cesario
was sure he was indeed speaking
to the mistress of the house,
he informed her that he had
come with a message from
the duke. He informed her
that she was very cruel not to
reciprocate his feelings of love.

Olivia, who was now completely under the spell of this charming page, did not want him to think she was cruel, so she declared that she knew the duke was a rather virtuous man, but still she could not love him. Cesario, in a bid to impress upon her the duke's love, said that if

he himself had loved
her like the duke
did, he would have
done all those things
the duke had spoken to
him about that morning. But
Olivia, hearing these words,
thought that they came from
the young page himself and

consequently fell
even more in
love with him.

Olivia now
wanted to send a
clear message to the
duke that she was
not in love with him,
so she asked Cesario
to convey her
message and told him that only
he could return to tell her how
the duke took the news. As soon
as Cesario left, Olivia felt a wild
energy overwhelm her, and she
started to imagine herself married
to the handsome Cesario.

Unable to contain
herself, Olivia decided to act

immediately. She sent one of
her own servants after Cesario
with a diamond ring, declaring
that he had left it behind. She
felt that this would give him a
suitable indication of
the love she felt for
him. And she almost
succeeded, because

when the servant caught up with
Cesario realized Olivia had fallen
in love with him. But Cesario
could only shake his head in
sorrow, because now he knew
that he could never reveal to the
duke that he was actually a girl,
nor could Olivia's love for the
fake Cesario ever be realized.

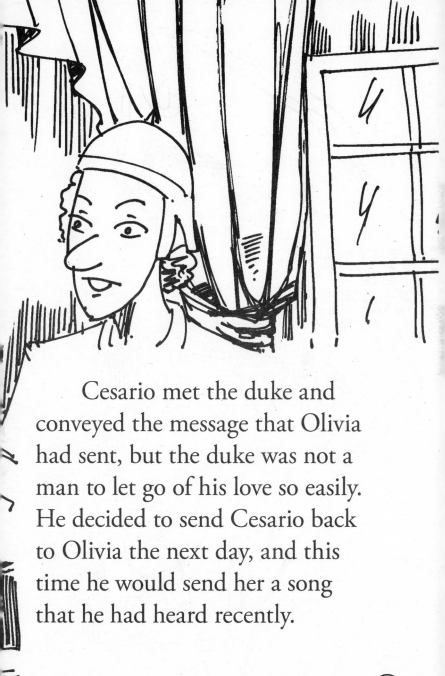

Cesario met the duke and
conveyed the message that Olivia
had sent, but the duke was not a
man to let go of his love so easily.
He decided to send Cesario back
to Olivia the next day, and this
time he would send her a song
that he had heard recently.

Come away, come away,
Death. And in sad cypress
let me be laid; Fly away,
fly away, breath, I am slain
by a fair cruel maid.

Cesario was truly moved by the song, and Orsino noticed the lovelorn look in his eyes. He immediately asked Cesario whether he too had fallen in love with someone. When Cesario confirmed that he had, the duke went on to ask his favorite page about the appearance of this damsel. Cesario merely replied that the person he was attracted to looked a lot like the duke. The duke felt sad upon hearing this,

because he felt that the woman he was talking about must be far older than Cesario himself and also rather dark. Little did he know that Cesario was actually

Viola, and the person he had described was the duke himself.

When Cesario made his second visit to Olivia, he was shown straight into her room. Olivia made it clear from the outset that she was not going to talk about the duke's proposals anymore. Rather, she

openly declared her love for
Cesario and spoke about how
she would die if he were to reject
her. Cesario was in a rather
embarrassing situation, and
merely said that he had resolved
never to love a woman and
took to his heels immediately.

While Cesario was walking
back toward the duke's castle,

he was confronted by another jilted lover of Olivia's. He at once challenged Cesario to a duel, thinking the young page to be another suitor. Cesario, being a woman, could not bring himself to fight with this man, and was about to declare that he was a woman in man's clothing when a passerby, seeing the plight, came over.

The man
started by telling
the other man that
Sebastian was a
dear friend of his
and, if he were to
cross swords with
him, he would be
forced to fight on
his behalf. The duel
was canceled, but
Cesario, or Viola,
was overjoyed to
hear the name of
her brother from
the lips of this man.
Obviously this man
knew her brother
and would be able to

lead her to him. But before Viola
could speak to him any further,

some guards came running toward them and arrested the man for a crime he had committed long ago. The man turned to Cesario and said, "Now do you see why I did not want to come back here? Look at the price I have had to pay for our friendship!"

Cesario declared that he had never seen the man before that moment, to which the stranger accused him of being ungrateful. The guards declared that this man had once wounded the duke's nephew in a sea-fight, the charge on which he was being arrested.

It was only later that Cesario learned the stranger's name was Antonio and that he was a sea-captain. He had found Sebastian

clinging to the mast after they were shipwrecked and drawn him into his own ship. Sebastian had asked to be taken to see the duke, and it was only because of their friendship that he had agreed to return to Illyria. He had asked Sebastian to wait for him at

the inn, but when he returned
he was not there. Therefore, he
had once again gone in search
of his friend. When he spotted
Cesario fighting with the other
man, and mistaking him to be
Sebastian—because after all

they were identical twins—
he had defended him.

Viola now wanted to
search for her brother, and felt
sure he was somewhere nearby.
Meanwhile, near the house of
Olivia, the real Sebastian was
confronted by the man who

had picked a fight with Cesario.
Sebastian, brave lad that he
was, refused to back down and
soon the two of them were in a
heated duel. Olivia came rushing
out and tried to stop them,
but she mistook Sebastian for
Cesario. Sebastian was rather
surprised by the courtesy of

this good lady, for this was the first time he had seen her.

Olivia tried to woo Cesario again, not knowing that the man in front of her was not Cesario but Sebastian. Sebastian did not turn down her efforts and was rather enamored by her beauty.

Olivia, thinking that Cesario
had changed his mind about
his love for her, immediately
arranged for a priest to come
and marry them. After they were
married, Sebastian informed
her that he should now go and
look for his friend Antonio

and tell him about his good
fortune. So he took his leave.

Soon after, the duke arrived
before Olivia, attended by
Cesario. Olivia started talking
to Cesario like a wife talks to
her husband, but Cesario denied
ever returning Olivia's love,

let alone getting married. A heartbroken Olivia immediately called the priest who had married them, who declared that he had indeed married them a couple of hours before.

Now the duke was furious with Cesario for taking away from him the only woman that he had ever loved. It was almost certain that the duke was about to kill Cesario, when suddenly, another Cesario burst upon the scene and started talking to Olivia as if he were her husband. Now there was total confusion all around. Sebastian and Viola kept looking at each other, unable to believe their eyes.

Finally, Viola declared to all present that he was not a man, but was actually Viola, Sebastian's twin sister. Only then did the whole thing start to make sense.

Finally, it was settled
that Sebastian would remain
married to Olivia. The duke
now remembered how Viola
kept talking to him about her
love and realized that it was not

a boy who had spoken to him, but a fair damsel. He finally agreed to Viola's proposals of love and offered to marry her.

The priest, who had been called upon as a witness, married Viola and Orsino immediately. Finally, all four of them were happy with their fate and laughed about all that had happened.